The ghost of the Bay House
JF Titterington

D1132604

112645

THE GHOST OF THE BAY HOUSE

From

'The Casebook of Simmons and Patterson'

Written by

Carl M Titterington

Carl M Titterington

The Ghost of the Bay House

Copyright © 2014 C M Titterington

All right reserved. No part of this work may be used, altered or reproduced by any means without the written permission of the author/publisher.

This book is a work of fiction. Any references to historical or ethnic events/traditions, real people or locales are used fictitiously.

Any resemblance to actual people or events should be considered coincidental as they are products of the author's imagination.

Book cover design © 2014 JDowell Designs

Edited by J M Titterington

Published by Anorak Publishing

Formatted by C M Titterington

ISBN-13: 978-1-494867416

ISBN-10: 1494867419

Anorak Publishing Company

Anorak Publishing Company was founded by R. Chapman with the aim to help aspiring writers publish and promote their works. For information, visit www.anorakpublishing.com.

Foreword from the Editor:

"The Ghost of the Bay House" began as a distraction, a way to pass the time while waiting for paths in life to develop a little more clearly. After meeting his wife, then his fiancée, and while waiting for his immigration to the US, the author found himself reading a collection of short stories by Sir Arthur Conan Doyle. For the first time in his life, he found himself devouring a book and suddenly he had an idea. He was soon to leave his hometown of Gosport, England and the village of Alverstoke where he had spent the better part of his life, but the creation of a pair of "consulting detectives" based in these very places proved a way to keep this world with him wherever he went. More than that, this book and those that follow it in "The Casebook of Simmons and Patterson" have given all of us a glimpse into a world we could never have imagined. While travelling in the land of Simmons and Patterson, we can encounter ghosts and mysteries, romance and daring, compassion and villainy. The author has written a work that he hopes will be accessible to all readers, including young people with dyslexia like himself. But this work is more than accessible, it is captivating. The characters, landscapes, and adventures within it draw in the reader in and keep the pages turning.

Enjoy your journey with us into the world of Simmons and Patterson and we'll see you soon. Best to start reading though. If I may paraphrase one of our favourite consulting detectives,

"Come readers, we have not a moment to lose."

Chapter One

It was a particularly warm evening in the east end of London. Men labored by the dockside as ships from across the Empire returned home to Britain. The sound of seagulls and horses echoed through the breezy air, the smell of sweat and the strong odor of fish lingered. Steam locomotives, which were a new arrival to the docklands, could be heard and their steam added to the smog of London. The voices of dockworkers competed with the aches of those tired souls returning from their voyages. It was not at all an uncommon sight to see sailors and soldiers' departing from vessels and this day was no exception.

As many did before him, Colonel Simmons stepped down the gangplank cautiously. He was a man of average height but of athletic stature and a wealthy gentleman who enjoyed outdoor pursuits, in particular sailing. To say that he was scared of falling and hurting himself would have been wrong. However, he wished to maintain an image of a competent leader in front of his troops. This sense of position and responsibility had not left him since the day he had earned his commission. Although he came from wealth he was determined to earn his position and the respect of those he led. He had earned this respect from his soldiers over the last few years in particular but it was something he was always working to maintain. His sense of honor was as important to him as his life. The army had been Simmons' life for many years since he was a young man but now, back in England, he would find himself challenged, more than any previous time in his career.

The Colonel on stepping off the gangplank paused. His eyes scanned the surroundings. I, his Orderly, a young man no more than twenty four years of age, stared at him with a puzzled looked but I should have known better after the years of serving by the Colonel's side. Simmons would often pause to study his whereabouts. He took note of every detail and this, although frustrating at times, was one trait his soldiers and I had been grateful for. On this occasion Simmons was taking note but he looked with purpose, a purpose that lasted just a few seconds as he spotted what he was looking for. Upon seeing his target he stepped off with intent at which I followed. Trawling through the puddles, which filled most of the quayside, Simmons came upon a man selling papers.

—

"Corporal, my coins if you would?" Simmons gestured.

"Yes sir." I replied.

Simmons paid the man and turning back towards the ship started to scan the headlines to see what had occurred in his absence. I looked on trying to catch a line here and there but Simmons flicked through the pages at quite a pace. It had always amazed me that my Colonel could take so much information on board in such a short space of time. Perhaps this was one of those skills that they taught officers or perhaps it was a trait that Simmons had perfected to the extent that it had saved the lives of his men on countless times. Just as I had started to scan one of the back pages, which was now on view, something odd happened or more precisely something usual didn't happen. Slightly worried, I asked,

"Sir? Is anything the matter?"

Simmons continued to stare, not a lost stare but more of an intrigued stare. A look that went further than the mere ink on the page. A look that searched between the lines for the clues that might just be the answer to his

Goodland Public Library
Goodland, KS 67735

worries. With no response from the Colonel I inquired again,

"Sir? Is there anything I can do for you?"

"Yes! Yes there is, fetch a cab at once," ordered Simmons.

I, who at this point was curious as to what the Colonel had seen, waved for a cab. It was only moments before a horse trotted over to our location pulling a standard carriage behind it. As the driver drew in line with us he shouted down from his seat,

"Where to governor?"

"Can you take us to…?", I replied instinctively but then paused. "What is our destination sir?" I enquired. Looking up. Simmons drew a deep breath and simple replied,

"The Seaside."

—

Chapter Two

As the cab ran along the rough country tracks, we sat quietly contemplating what lay before us. I puzzled about what it was that my good Colonel had seen in that newspaper, which seaside town might our destination be and what his plan of action was. He was certainly no stranger to action or adventure but this seemed different somehow. As we sat, both of us in our own thoughts, the Colonel lit his pipe and started to puff away on it. His expression was one of a calm man but at the same time a man who was clearly thinking. After a moment of consideration as what to say and clearing my throat, I made the bold decision to break the silence.

"Sir, may I ask, what was it that you saw in that newspaper?"

Colonel Simmons looked up. Removing his pipe from his lips he said in a calm and reasoning voice,

"What did I see? Well, quite simply a puzzle, a mystery. A terrible occurrence, which seems to have landed itself close to the shores of Stokes Bay."

"Stokes Bay Sir?" I asked with an enquiring voice.

The Colonel looked at me as if to suggest a lack of geographical knowledge. Being from the Yorkshire Dales I was more accustomed to the rolling hills than to the coasts of Hampshire.

"Stokes Bay is a little way down the coast from Portsmouth harbor. By a small village named Alverstoke. A quaint little place. Much desirable to many a rich man from London seeking to escape the compact and filthy environment," Simmons explained.

I was grateful, as I had been on many occasions, for the Colonel's patient manner. There had been many lessons I had learnt since joining him at the age of sixteen. The quality of my reading and written word had been one of the many and for this I was indebted to him.

Although Colonel Simmons had been good enough as to explain where our destination would be, it still left a desire to know more brewing inside of me. As a result of this curiosity, which I can only describe as an itch failing to settle, I continued to enquire as to the answers of my other previous questions.

"Pardon me for asking sir but what is this terrible

—

occurrence you speak of?"

"It seems to be that a fisherman has gone missing," answered Simmons.

"A fisherman sir? What has that got to do with us? Surely it must be the duty of the village constable to discover the whereabouts of the missing man." I questioned with an even deeper sense of confusion.

"My dear Patterson, there is more to this than simply a missing man," the Colonel calmly stated. "No body has yet been found and there are further reports from other fisherman of very peculiar happenings in the area."

"Peculiar happenings sir?" I asked in a more spooked manner.

I had seen many things while serving with Colonel Simmons but I had never heard him refer to any of these as 'peculiar'. This word did not fit his way of thinking. The Colonel was a man of logic and deduction. To suggest that any event or incident could not be explained by reason was too much for him.

The cab turned a corner and a dreadful sound of a strong, wild wind blew through the main compartment. The air turned cold and for a moment I felt uneasy. Glancing out of the window I could see that our journey had brought us now to the seaside but not a seaside that I had seen in Egypt. No, this was a seaside, which had not long turned from the pleasant summer retreat to a hard-hitting wintery coast. As the wind swept up the shore, the waves lashed against the rough stony beach, which seemingly was our only defense from Poseidon's waves. I shuddered at the gloomy, dreary surroundings.

I guessed we must be nearing our destination and so considered it wise to find out what my Colonel had planned.

"Sir, what is it you plan to do about this whole entirely puzzling incident?"

As the cab pulled up outside a long row of beautiful white town houses, Simmons looked on pleasingly and then turning his head back towards me to respond to my curiosity he answered,

"I intend to find the Ghost of the Bay House!"

—

Chapter Three

After securing lodgings for a few days we made our way down the crescent past a picturesque little garden. It was sheltered from the wind by tall evergreens and the floor covered by crisp orange leaves as if carpeted. On the other side was the row of beautiful white townhouses. The architecture only suggested further the wealth of the area.

As we got closer to the end of the garden I asked of my Colonel,

"Sir, by any chance are we on our way to the beach?"

"You are quite correct Corporal and as you are probably wondering as to what we might be doing there I shall enlighten you further," stated the Colonel. "I wish to look at the area from the fisherman's point of view and if we get the chance I wish to speak with some of them."

As we reached the sight of the sea we turned our path along the beach and were faced not only with the strong, fearsome winds but also the delightful sight of the sun beginning to set. The light painted the dusk sky with fiery reds and oranges bringing a sense of beauty upon what otherwise could have been described as a harsh wilderness. For one of a nervous or even frightened disposition the red and orange sky could have acted as a warning of danger but not for Colonel Simmons.

As I looked down the coastline I could see the water's edge was lined with fishermen and their lanterns. However, as my gaze moved further down the shore I saw quite a gap in this seemingly endless line of fisherman.

"Sir..."

"Yes. I see Patterson," interrupted Simmons.

"But why the gap sir?" I questioned, as yet something else peculiar seemed to have arisen.

"I should imagine it has something to do with our friend, the Ghost, but let us hold back the speculation until we have the facts to guide us to the truth," answered Simmons in a calm fashion.

We continued along the beach until we reached the gap in the line. Simmons paused as he had just a day or two ago on the quayside of the London docklands. His eyes

—

scanned the surroundings. Firstly, out to sea, then along the coast. East and west and upon taking in what he saw he turned his attention north, inland.

Whilst my Colonel took in all there was to take in and more, I decided to observe the area in order to assist in what little way I could. I started by looking north in which direction I saw mostly trees but as I scanned, the vastness of the almost forest like image, my eyes caught a glance of a house like shape through the tree line. I wondered for a moment to who might live there. They must have some wealth about them to own such a place. I started up the beach to take a closer look but as I did a small group of men heading towards us caught my eye. Then one of them spoke out,

"Can I help you gentlemen?" shouted one of the men.

Simmons halted in his observation and froze. I decided to take it upon myself to answer.

"Good evening, we're just here looking for…"

"We're just looking for the best place to fish," interrupted Simmons. "Is this part of the shore particularly poor for fishing?" he asked.

"No, this part is as good as any along the bay," explained the man.

It was clear by their appearance that these men were fishermen, however, we clearly were not. I was therefore confused as to why Colonel Simmons should infer that we were. These men must have known that we weren't who we implied. I stood puzzled and listened to see where Simmons was leading the conversation.

"May I ask then gentleman why this stretch of shore is abandoned?" enquired Simmons.

The two fishermen glanced at each other with a look of worry. After returning their view back to Colonel Simmons and I the second fisherman swallowed nervously and said,

"You can't be from around these parts if you're asking that," the fisherman exclaimed with a tone of fear in his voice. "'ave you not 'eard about the Ghost?"

—

"A Ghost?" questioned Simmons.

"Yes! A Ghost, up in the 'ouse!" cried the first fisherman.

"Has anyone seen this Ghost?" asked Simmons as his plan came to light.

"Well I 'aven't but my mate John 'as," said the first fisherman defensively.

"And don't forget Collins!" interrupted the second fisherman.

"Where are these men at the present time?" enquired Simmons carefully.

"Well, John is down the beach a bit fishing and Collins, well …if you 'aven't 'eard he went missin' a week ago," explained the second fisherman. "They 'ad both wandered up to the Bay 'ouse to 'ave a closer look. That's when they saw it. There 'ave been rumors circulating for a few months and they were just itching to find out if they were true. John said that they saw it and at that point he said they should leave but Collins, no Collins couldn't believe it, he 'ad to take a closer look. You see Collins 'ad spent time at sea and he'd seen a lot but…" the fisherman paused.

"Anyhow, who did you say you were?" asked the first man in a slightly aggressive tone. "You can't be the police cause they don't believe us and the reporters 'ave already asked us for the details. So who are you?"

Simmons, without a moment's hesitation, answered, "We are an interested third party shall we say."

"You've not been sent by that Mr. Bowles 'ave you?" the second man asked suspiciously.

"Mr. Bowles?" I asked, jumping in.

"Yeah, the gentleman who's been trying to buy the Bay 'ouse now for ages," explained the first man.

"Trying to buy Bay House you say," Simmons mumbled to himself. "How very interesting. I'm afraid we are not associates of Mr. Bowles but may I enquire as to how long he has been trying to buy the house?" Simmons asked, clearly making a mental note.

"Well let's see, it must be at least three or four

—

months," explained the first man.

"I wish to thank you gentlemen, you have been of great help to us but may I ask upon you one more favor? Just a simple question. Who might be the current owner?" asked Colonel Simmons.

"Ah, well that would be Dr. Brown's daughters. Unfortunately, God rest 'is soul, the good Doctor Brown passed away a year ago. He used the 'ouse as an extension of the Naval College," explained the fisherman.

"As in the Naval College at Clarence?" Simmons asked quickly.

"Yeah that's the one!" said the second man.

"Where might we find John and these ladies?" Simmons asked.

"Well, John will be where he is most nights, at the Village Home," the fisherman said smirking. "The ladies are staying in a cottage along the Avenue, just down the lane from the church."

"Thank you again for all your help!" I shouted whilst catching up to the Colonel who had already started to make his way towards the tree line.

Simmons walked briskly towards the tree line where I had been looking earlier. So fast was his pace that I was almost running to catch up. As I tried to catch up I cried out,

"Sir, why so fast?"

Simmons in his usual controlled tone answered, "I'm afraid the light is fading and I want to get a closer look before it is no more than a mere silhouette in the moonlight sky."

As we drew closer we could see the house itself. It was a beautifully built house with a lovely veranda overlooking a garden, which although becoming slightly over grown must at one time have been taken very good care of. Simmons's eyes scanned the property looking for every detail that he could note before the light of the dusk sky faded. It appeared to me that there was very little to see. There were no broken windows. No lights on and certainly no sign of any ghost. I pondered as to whether

—

this may be just a drunk fisherman's tale but my Colonel from the look of focus upon his face clearly did not believe it to be so.

"It is getting dark." Simmons exclaimed. "Come Patterson, it is time for a drink."

"Music to my ears sir," I replied with a sense of jest.

"We shall retire from this place to the Village Home. I believe there is more to learn before the night is over," explained Simmons, with a determined voice and no jest at all.

Chapter Four

The smell of wood burning fires filled the air, small terrace houses and cottages lined the lanes of the small quaint village. As we made our way towards one of the larger buildings in the village we could hear the laughter of a group of men and the creaking of a sign, swinging in the wind. We had found the Village Home and so headed inside.

Colonel Simmons led the way into the busy room. As I stepped in I was hit by the smell of spirits, ales and smoke that drifted through the warm air. The roaring fire in the centre of the room gave the place a homey feel and warmed the bones of the local fishermen who were gathered around a group of tables in the corner. The bar was busy with people from the village, drinking and talking, telling jokes and remembering stories of old. The public house was full, as on many nights, of various groups from the local community, however, they all had one thing in common, they were locals. As the door closed behind us it was as if every set of eyes in the room turned their attention upon my Colonel and I. Conversations paused as questioning, puzzled faces turned to discover who these

—

new men were.

After taking in his surroundings and scanning the room for every little detail, Simmons made his way towards the bar. Feeling uncomfortable standing by myself I moved swiftly over to the bar to join my Colonel. As the group at the bar parted, Colonel Simmons was greeted by the barman.

"Good evening. How can I help you gentlemen?" asked the barman.

"Good evening, I shall have a glass of Taylor's Port if you have it. And for you Patterson?" the Colonel asked.

"A pint of ale, if I may sir?" I replied humbly.

Taking the drinks from the barman and having paid we made our way over to a free table, which was quite hard to find due to the volume of people occupying the room. After taking our seats I took a sip of my drink and on doing so turned to Colonel Simmons and asked,

"Sir, what is it we are looking for in here?" I presumed, due to my Colonel's gentlemanly nature that we couldn't be here simply for a drink. If that had have been the case then it would have been more likely for us to retire to our lodgings.

"Well Patterson, if you believe that the sole purpose for this visit is not a mere drink you would be correct. I believe that some important information lies within these four walls that will help us with this mystery," Simmons explained.

I was unsure about whom or what my Colonel could be talking about but the atmosphere was certainly not a comfortable one. As we sat and scanned the room I felt a chill go down my spine. The air suddenly felt cooler and then warm again. I could hear the wild gusts of wind, blowing outside, some tree branches knocking against the window. I felt as if I was being watched, indeed as if we were both being watched. However, this could be partly explained as we were strangers in this very 'local' public house. To calm myself I thought it wise to look to my Colonel who as in so many situations appeared composed and focused.

"So where are we going to find this information sir?" I

—

asked with an unsteadied tone.

"It is not a case of us finding the information but the information finding us," explained Colonel Simmons, with an air of certainty.

At that moment I caught the shaggy figure of one of the fisherman out of the corner of my eye. He walked over to our table and addressed us.

"Excuse me gentlemen. I heard you were down at the beach earlier talking to some of the others. I also heard you were asking about the Bay House."

"That's correct," answered Simmons

"And who might you be?" I asked.

"My name is John. I was with Collins the night he went missing. When I heard that two gentlemen were interested in what happened I was worried. However, my friends told me that you weren't working for Mr. Bowles and you definitely weren't from the police or the newspapers. I thought it was important for me to come talk to you," explained the fisherman while nervously biting his nails.

"Well John, it's very good of you to come and speak with us. May I begin by asking you why you were worried that we were under the employment of Mr. Bowles?" enquired Simmons.

"Well to be truthful, I don't like the man. He has men who work for him and they have, well let's say they have convinced men to make decisions that work to Mr. Bowles' advantage. He wants the Bay House and I... well I wouldn't be surprised if he is behind Collins' disappearance" stuttered the fisherman.

"Can you tell us what you saw the other night at the Bay House?" I asked, hoping to find out more about the Ghost itself.

"Well... we... we saw... we saw it," John said with a fearful tone. "We saw the Ghost!"

"Where did you see the Ghost?" Simmons asked further.

"He was up in the room above the veranda, but then

—

he wasn't and then he suddenly appeared in one of the downstairs rooms at the other end of the house. It got me all shaken up but Collins thought something was up. He told me he wanted to take a closer look but I told him that we couldn't." explained the fisherman who by this point had sweat upon his brow.

"What did the Ghost look like?" continued Simmons.

"I saw a figure and a bright light. The figure was practically shining," exclaimed John.

"Very interesting. Well thank you for your time but finally may I enquire as to why you told Mr. Collins that you couldn't take a closer look?" Simmons finished.

"Simple. The House has been boarded up for months," stated the fisherman.

At that, the shaky fisherman looked around nervously, stood up, and rejoined his friends in the corner. Colonel Simmons and I finished our drinks and then decided to retire for the night. I grabbed my long coat and, following the colonel, left through the door, which we previously entered.

The weather was still of an aggressive nature. The wind was blowing in an easterly direction and as we walked towards the Crescent, where our lodgings were to be found, it started to rain. Due to this our pace quickened and on reaching the house we opened the front door to be greeted by the landlady. She kindly took our long coats from us and hung them up to dry. We then proceeded to the drawing room to have a nightcap before resting for the mysteries that would surely face us the following day.

While sitting in what was a very comfortable armchair I asked of my Colonel, "Sir, it appears to me that all we have heard today has only made this mystery all the more unusual. The fishermen seemed jumpy about the Bay House and even John didn't explain what happened to Collins. And now along with this ghost business we have the suspicious Mr. Bowles."

Colonel Simmons took a sip of his drink and with a thoughtful pause he then replied to my confusion. "It is more unusual and mysterious to someone who is blinded

—

by the fearful thoughts of some supernatural occurrence. However, when one takes this abnormal factor out of the equation for a moment and looks at the facts, the mystery becomes clearer and more logical. Tomorrow should wrap up the case in my mind. I believe we should pay Dr. Brown's daughters a visit to discover the extent of the situation concerning the Bay House."

"Very well, sir. If there is nothing else, I shall retire to bed," I said, just prior to yawning.

"No Patterson, nothing else. I shall retire myself. Good night," Simmons said.

"Good night, sir," I stated as I left the drawing room and headed for my room.

As I got ready for bed and slipped under the covers I could hear the rains smashing against the side of the house. I lay in bed pleased to be out of the weather and a sense of safety came over me. It had been a few years since I had worried about the rain; the places I had been sandstorms had been the biggest concern. I attempted to get to sleep with some success. It must have been at least a couple of hours that went past before I was roughly awakened. Out of nowhere I heard moans and groans of a frightful nature. I turned in my bed to listen more closely and then to my fear I jumped at the sound of a blood-curling scream. I yelled out helplessly,

"SIR!"

Chapter Five

I was worried as to what might happen if I left the safety of my bed. However, a sense of loyalty came over me. If in fact my Colonel was in trouble or danger, I couldn't hide away and let something happen to him. After getting out of bed and putting on my gown I headed for the hall landing. Moving slowly, with a candle in one hand, I crept towards Colonel Simmons' room. As I got closer I could hear my Colonel shouting,

"No... No...!"

Hearing him, in what I presumed was a conflict; I dashed to his door and opened it. What I saw next shocked me. I could not believe what I was seeing. Huddled in the corner of the room was a figure, a dark reclusive shell of a man. I crept closer and as I did the man flung his arms up over his head in a guarding action. I held the candle closer to see whom it was and to my horror I saw my colonel.

"Colonel Simmons? Colonel... are you ok?" I asked caringly. The colonel continued to shake in a scared manner. I reached out a hand and placed it on his shoulder, attempting to comfort him. At that moment my

Colonel sharply turned his head up and towards me. His eyes bold and piercing, a look that went through me but also cried out for help. I put the candle on the side and embraced Colonel Simmons. He continued to shake but as I held him he started to withdraw from what can only be described from my observation as a terrible nightmare.

After calming the Colonel down I helped him into bed and, pulling the covers over him, I moved back to keep a safe watch over him for a while. He settled and after a short while was asleep. When I was sure that he would rest well I left and returned to my room. As I got into my bed, thoughts went through my head of what could have caused my Colonel to react in this way. What was on his mind? Colonel Simmons on the whole had always appeared to me to be a man in control of himself and his emotions. I fell asleep considering the possibilities behind the night's disturbance.

The morning arrived somewhat faster than hoped. As I arose from my bed in a half woken state, I reflected upon the events of the last few days. I believed in Colonel Simmons' ability and the likelihood that he would be able

—

to solve this mystery. However, many things had happened that I certainly could not explain. Today was going to be an important day for the case and secretly I was pleased. I had seen and faced many worrying situations with Colonel Simmons but never a ghost. It sent shivers down my spine.

After having a wash and getting dressed I walked to my Colonel's room and gave the door a couple of knocks. I was slightly surprised to have not received a response from the room; however, I presumed that the Colonel was still asleep. With the events of the night in the forefront of my mind I thought to check on him. I entered the room slowly as to not awaken my Colonel from his much-needed rest but to my surprise he was nowhere to be seen. His bed was made as neatly as one would expect from an army officer. Perhaps he was already down eating breakfast. I therefore proceeded downstairs and on entering the dining room I again could not see my Colonel. At that moment I began to panic. Where was he? Had anything happened to him? Should I have stayed in his room to watch over him? I quickly headed for the front door, grabbing my coat from the coat stand, my hand reached for the door handle and at that moment the door opened. I jumped with shock and

I was confronted with the calm, controlled face of Colonel Simmons.

"Good morning Patterson. Did you sleep well?" Simmons asked in a collected fashion.

"Good morning…sir," I said in a confused tone. "I slept… fairly well sir. And how did you sleep sir?"

"I slept well. Thank you Patterson," Simmons replied plainly. "Shall we have some breakfast now? That walk has brought a hunger upon my stomach."

"Yes sir," I said leading the way to the dining room.

We sat down and poured some tea, which had been put out by the landlady. As we began to talk, our landlady appeared and asked if we cared for some toast and jam. We gratefully agreed and continued our conversation.

"May I ask sir where your walk took you this morning?" I enquired.

"I had a thought upon awakening this morning that we had not been able to have as thorough a look at the Bay House and the surrounding area last night as I would have

—

hoped to. I ventured along the beach to the spot in the trees from which we had observed the house last night. After seeing that it was fairly well secured I moved along the perimeter until I came upon a small, rather lovely house. The name over the door was Alverbank House. After making a mental note of the surrounding area I walked to the village where I picked up today's paper, which certainly holds some interesting news, I must say. I then commissioned the paperboy to deliver a message to the daughters of Dr. Brown. A reply returned with the paper boy accepting my request to meet with them at ten this morning," Colonel Simmons explained thoroughly.

"I see sir. Did you learn anything else that will help us solve this mystery?" I asked.

"The mystery is certainly becoming clearer but I am confident that after this morning we shall clear this up finally," Simmons answered confidently.

"Sir..." I stuttered.

"Yes Patterson?" Simmons replied.

"I do not mean to be rude but what happened last night?" I enquired in a respectful but inquisitive manner.

"Last night?" Simmons asked with slight sense of panic.

"Yes sir! I heard shouting and yelling. When I went to your room, I found you curled up in the corner as if something terrible had happened," I explained.

"Oh, I see," replied Simmons, who quite clearly was upset at the fact that I had seen him in this state.

"I'm sorry sir. I didn't mean to cause insult or upset," I quickly added. I didn't want my Colonel to feel ashamed or embarrassed, I simply wanted to discover the origins of the events of last night and help if indeed I could.

"You haven't insulted me, Patterson. In fact as upset and embarrassed as I am, there is a small part of me that is relieved. This is not the first time that I have been overcome by such grief and fear. As much as it burdens me to say it, it is caused by nightmares," Simmons explained.

"If I may ask sir, what are the nightmares about?" I asked cautiously.

—

"They are mostly memories. In particular a battle that has not passed more than 11 years to this day. Prior to joining the York and Lancaster regiment in the winter of 1883, I was a young officer in the 66th of Foot and then part of the Royal Berkshire regiment. We were posted to the south of Afghanistan, just west of Kandahar. The battle in question was fought as a result of a dash made to take a small village called Maiwand before the Afghans could. However, due to our late departure from our previous location we were left exposed in open ground, which the Afghan army took full advantage of. The following battle was bloody and we were forced to retreat. Outnumbered and out gunned, some small groups, including the one that I was attached to, decided to hold our ground to give the others more time to fall back. I, in the end and to my disgrace was ordered to take my group and rejoin the others. I did so and the fate of the others was decided. They fell to the swords of the enemy. And since the battle of Tamai, which you will remember, I have on many occasions in my dreams relived that moment and thought about what else could have been done to have saved them," Simmons described in a clinical yet somewhat emotional manner.

"Sir, there was nothing you could do. If you had stayed you also would have been killed. You saved your men and that was important," I empathized.

"What do you know about leadership? How can you know what I should have done? You weren't there!" Colonel Simmons exclaimed with anger.

There was an awkward silence as I retreated back into myself feeling truly rebuked. Simmons then on taking a deep breath and collecting himself spoke,

"I am deeply sorry Patterson. I spoke aggressively and in an improper manner to you. I was upset and lost once again to the haunting experiences of that day. I do beg your forgiveness on the matter."

"Sir, no forgiveness is required. I spoke out of turn and in a manner that no Corporal should address an officer in. It is I who should beg your forgiveness," I replied, hoping to settle the situation so we might as continue on the good relations that had been built over the many years since Major Simmons had joined the York and

Lancaster regiment and then subsequently had been promoted to a Lieutenant-Colonel and finally Colonel.

"My dear Patterson, you have been of splendid support and no more loyal man could I find. Thank you," Simmons said with a soft tone of voice.

We drank our tea and ate what was a delicious breakfast. As we sat, admiring the lovely sunshine beaming through the beautiful bay window of the dining room, the landlady entered the room. Taking the used plates and cups from our table, she informed us that our cab had arrived and was waiting for us at the front.

"Splendid! I must remember to tip our driver, he has impeccable timing. Patterson our coats if you would. We do not wish to be late for our appointment with the daughters of the late Dr. Brown."

After a short journey from our lodgings in the Crescent, we turned in to a rather large road lined with beautiful oak trees. They created something of a canopy over this aged road. As we descended down the road, I saw the splendor of many a fine house sparsely spread out. The cab began to slow and as it did the thatched roof of a humble little cottage caught my eye. Its awe was masked by the many rose bushes that guarded the perimeter of its majestic garden. If indeed this was the residence of the daughters of the late Dr. Brown, then they certainly knew how to keep a wonderful garden.

I stepped out of the cab followed by Colonel Simmons. We walked towards the cottage captivated by the scent of the well-nurtured roses of the garden. I opened the gate and my Colonel led the way down the garden path to the door. Pulling the bell, we waited. After a short wait the door opened and a lovely young lady who was more than likely in her mid-twenties greeted us.

"Good morning, gentlemen," the lady answered.

"Good morning. My name is Colonel Simmons and this is my orderly Corporal Patterson. We have an appointment to see the daughters of the late Dr. Brown," Simmons explained.

"Pleased to meet you Colonel Simmons, Corporal Patterson. My name is Emily Brown, please follow me."

—

We followed Miss Brown through a small hallway to a reception room that housed a small table with a few chairs. On the table was a teapot and four cups beautifully placed on saucers. As we took a seat Miss Brown poured out four fresh cups of tea.

"Colonel Simmons, Corporal Patterson, I would like to introduce you to my sister Sylvia Brown," Emily Brown said whilst handing us a cup of tea each.

"A pleasure to meet you Miss Brown. It is very kind of you to receive us," Colonel Simmons exclaimed.

"Colonel Simmons, if you can help solve the mystery surrounding our father's house then my sister and I will be more than willing to reward you for your help," Sylvia insisted with a sense of frustration in her voice.

"We would like to ask you both some questions if you would not mind," I stated.

"Of course, Corporal Patterson," Emily answered.

"Miss Brown, would you be so kind as to explain to us the situation regarding your father's house?" Simmons asked inquisitively.

"After our father died he left the house to my sister and I. However, over the last year the costs of keeping the house have mounted. We could not afford to keep the staff on let alone live there. We had the house locked and boarded up and we have been searching for a buyer ever since. Unfortunately, due to our father having some unsettled accounts, a local magistrate ruled that if the Bay House was not sold within a year, it would be sold to Mr. Bowles in order to settle our father's debts," Emily explained.

"Mr. Bowles, as in the Mr. Andrew Bowles, member of the local council?" Simmons asked.

"That is correct, Colonel Simmons. I dislike the man. He made some very inappropriate advances on Sylvia and our father thought very ill of Mr. Bowles," Emily said with a bitter tone.

"I'm sorry to hear that Miss Brown," I said with a sympathetic voice.

"Miss Brown, I am certain as to whom is behind the Ghost of the Bay House but would it be possible to have a closer look of the house, just for curiosities sake?" Colonel

—

Simmons asked in a very sure manner.

"Certainly Colonel Simmons we can go now if that would suit you both," Sylvia said rising from her seat.

"Excellent! My cab can take us there. Patterson would you mind telling the driver our intentions whilst the ladies collect their coats?" Simmons asked.

As I got up from my seat and headed towards the hallway I answered, "Certainly sir. I will let him know our destination." As I left the house I could hear the sound of the horse from the cab, I could smell the scent of the roses and I felt the breeze on my face. I walked down the garden path and out through the gate. I explained to the cab driver that we would be going to the Bay House. I opened the door to the cab and opened out the folding metal step. As I did, the ladies - escorted by Colonel Simmons - came down the path and out to the cab. I assisted the ladies up and into the cab and once in, I returned the step to its folded position. My Colonel and I then entered the cab and closed the door.

After a short journey we arrived at the gates of the Bay House. I was asked by Miss Brown to step out and unlock the large black iron gates that joined the beautiful stone walls that made up the perimeter of the grounds to the house. After reentering the cab, we made our way down the long drive towards the main house. The drive was lined with trees that gave the house a grand impression. We pulled up and exited the cab in turn, myself followed by the Brown daughters and finally Colonel Simmons. I was immediately taken back by the stunning stone work which made up the front of the house. As the cab pulled away towards the stables, I moved towards the main entrance with Miss Emily Brown. She took a key from her pocket and unlocked the large wooden door. It swung open with a groaning creak. I was about to enter the house when Colonel Simmons called out,

"Wait...," he turned his attention from scanning the building to the front door, "we must tread carefully, there is evidence within that door."

Colonel Simmons led the way in and walked cautiously. He scanned from side to side, along the floor

—

and up the walls. Everything looked as if it should. It appeared as if it had been left alone for a considerable amount of time. He paused,

"Miss Brown, is there anything that looks out of place to you?

"Everything looks as we left it," Sylvia answered.

We continued to explore the rooms of the house. On doing so we found many pieces of furniture covered with sheets. The decoration was beautiful and inferred the splendor that was held by Dr. Brown's residence in it's prime.

As we advanced down the hallway towards the master staircase Colonel Simmons stopped. Looking down he saw something, something small enough that I could not see it. But there was more. Simmons crouched and moved forward, continuing to observe the small pieces of evidence.

"Hmmm, very interesting…" Colonel Simmons exclaimed.

I pondered for a moment as to what Colonel Simmons might have seen but before I had a chance to ask he was moving on, down the hallway.

"Miss Brown could I awfully trouble you to show me to the room above the veranda?" Colonel Simmons asked.

"The Morning room? Certainly, it is up the master staircase and to the left," Emily Brown answered.

We made our way up the staircase. At the top we turned left and went into the room on the right. Colonel Simmons paused and turning to the ladies he asked,

"Ladies, would you mind just giving us a moment to examine the room properly?"

"By all means."

We entered the room and began to look for anything that did not belong. Colonel Simmons moved round the room clockwise from the door. I, on the other hand, decided to take a look out of the window, which led to the balcony. I moved towards the glass door that opened out to the balcony but as I drew closer I picked up the smell of something strong. I looked around hurriedly to see if I could find the origin of this potent fragrance. My eyes scanned the floor quickly and then I stopped. Returning my gaze to the beautiful carpet I saw something out of place. On closer inspection there appeared to be a stain. Turning my head towards my Colonel I called out,

"Colonel Simmons! Come quickly!"

As the Colonel moved over to join me, I took a knee to further my inspection. I started by taking a sniff of the stained area of the carpet. It was definitely the same smell. I then took off my glove and touched the stain with my index finger. It was damp.

"Sir, what do you make of this," I asked.

"Well, it appears that someone has been here recently and by the smell our guest was carrying a paraffin lamp. This stain must be a splash mark from the lamp. I do believe, Patterson, that we have the answer to our friend the Ghost. We have seen everything we need to, let us return downstairs," Simmons explained.

At that we turned and exited the room. As we left the room we asked the ladies if it might be possible to further examine downstairs. We followed the ladies down the master staircase, past the drawing room and just before we entered the foyer, I noticed Colonel Simmons stop. I turned to see why my Colonel had stopped.

"Sir, is everything well?"

"There is a smell here, Patterson," Simmons replied.

"The same smell as in the morning room," I asked.

"No. This is a stronger smell. A most evil smell that I have not had the displeasure of smelling for quite some time. It is a smell that no man can forget once he has smelt it one fateful time."

Colonel Simmons started to creep slowly, continually sniffing like a hound trying to find his prey. Coming upon a door Colonel Simmons motioned to me,

"It's coming from behind this door."

Simmons slowly opened the door and led the way down a small spiral staircase. As we descended a cold feeling came upon me. This time it was not due to fear but due to a drop in temperature. We entered what appeared

—

to be the servants' access to the kitchens. One could only presume that this was the corridor that the servants would come along from the kitchen to serve the food to the dining room. Lighting a candle that was on a plinth beside the wall, we continued to search. Our enquiry brought us to two side rooms. The smell, which by this point was stronger than it had been upstairs, led us to the back of the room where we could see a pair of bread ovens.

"Perhaps Patterson the ladies should not be present for this," Simmons said calmly but compassionately.

I suggested to the ladies that they take a step back and on doing so rejoined Colonel Simmons to discover what the ovens had to hide. Simmons turned the large iron handle which held the doors of the oven shut. I pulled on one of the door handles as Simmons pulled the other. I could not believe my eyes. How could he have gotten here?

"Patterson, we have found our missing fisherman, we have found Collins," Simmons said in a jubilant tone.

Puzzled by my Colonel's tone I questioned,

"Sir, how can you be so thrilled about this discovery?"

"Can you not see Patterson, we are so ever closer to solving this mystery," Simmons exclaimed like a proud schoolboy.

Slightly confused and puzzled as to whether the second room might also hold a clue to the mystery I left the first room and moved towards the second. As I came to the entrance of the other room I paused. I thought I could feel something on my cheek. Could it be? Calling out I said,

"Sir, there is something here."

Colonel Simmons moved swiftly to my position and on arriving he paused. There was a cool breeze coming from the second room. We moved in slowly and found several wine racks covered in dust. On the left side of the room was a rack that was six foot in height, much taller than the others. We followed the breeze to the large rack and started to examine it.

"Patterson, I believe this wine rack is concealing some sort of entrance."

On feeling round the edge, Colonel Simmons

—

discovered some hinges. I was not having as much luck but on taking a step back I saw something so obvious I couldn't believe we had missed it. There was only one bottle of wine resting in the rack towards the right side, a bottle singular in shape and design. I gestured to Colonel Simmons at which he proceeded to place his hand on the neck of the bottle. On doing so he lifted it upwards. Immediately we heard a click and the wine rack swung open towards us.

"Patterson," said the Colonel, "I believe it's time we invited the police to join our little party."

Chapter Six

The police arrived to take the body away. Accompanying them was an inspector by the name of Gaunless. Richard A. Gaunless had been with the police force from its creation. He had been a 'Peeler' in London for a few years before moving to become a detective in the south. His team was in charge of investigating murders and other serious crimes in the southern part of the county of Hampshire.

On arriving at the Bay House, Inspector Gaunless interviewed Miss Emily and Sylvia Brown. They explained the situation and stated that Colonel Simmons and myself had been very kind to offer our assistance to the mystery of the Ghost of the Bay House and of the missing fisherman. At this point the inspector made his way over to us.

"Colonel Simmons, I presume?" the inspector asked.

"You are indeed correct, sir. And who might I have the privilege of speaking to?" replied Colonel Simmons.

"My name is Inspector Gaunless of the south Hampshire Constabulary. I lead a team of men who

—

investigate murders and other serious crimes," the inspector stated. "It appears clear to me that this fisherman died whilst breaking in to the property. I presume that the Ghost was just a story by the local fisherman to keep people away so they could plunder the property for valuables."

"I'm afraid, inspector, that is not the case," said the Colonel quite firmly. "The fisherman did not break into the house. You are correct about the creation of a story about the Ghost but it was not the fisherman who created it. I have been quite sure about the mystery surrounding this house for some time now and this most recent discovery has only cemented what I know to be the truth. It is important inspector that you follow my instruction to the letter if you wish to catch the persons behind this crime."

"I'm sorry. I must protest to your statement. How is it that you are so sure of incident that has occurred? I am a professional and no matter how high a commission you might hold in Her Majesty's Army, this does not give you authority on this matter," exclaimed the Inspector in a more aggressive tone.

"My dear Inspector, it is not a question of seniority but a question of the facts that we know. I shall explain all in due course but it is important that we move quickly," Simmons said with a tone of insistence.

Looking as if he had no choice in the matter, the Inspector asked of Colonel Simmons

"What is it you would have me do, sir?"

"Firstly, we need to send for Mr. Bowles on behalf of Mr. Chambers. It is important that Mr. Bowles arrives at the residence of Mr. Chambers at the Alverbank before the police arrive. I shall send along with you my orderly Corporal Patterson. I will instruct him upon the rest of the plan," stated Colonel Simmons.

"I understand," replied the Inspector helplessly.

With an air of confusion, Inspector Gaunless left us and instructed a policeman to send for Mr. Bowles on behalf of Mr. Chambers. Meanwhile Colonel Simmons instructed me on the next part of the plan and upon

—

completion I left to join the police.

After a short period of time, Inspector Gaunless, myself and a few constables took a police wagon along the beach to the residence of Mr. Chambers. The wagon along with the police kept out of sight whilst I kept a look out for the arrival of Mr. Bowles. Waiting, I thought about my time with the army. It had been a simple life. I had seen parts of the world, which I had never dreamed of seeing. However, foreign worlds were not England, they were not where I wanted to be. I began to listen to the waves gently lapping against the stones of the beach. The beautiful sunshine beaming down made for a peaceful spot. I felt myself start to drift into a dose but all of a sudden I heard the sound of hooves trotting along the road. I hid myself behind an evergreen bush so as not to be seen and as the carriage passed over the small bridge into the courtyard of the Alverbank house I saw an important man inside. It must be Mr. Bowles, I thought to myself. After seeing the man enter the house I came out from behind the bush and signaled to the police to make their move. I walked up over the bridge and met them at the entrance to the beautiful house.

Inspector Gaunless stepped out of the wagon and joined me to ring the bell of the house. A stocky man with a beard answered the door after a moment. He looked as if he could handle himself in a fight but luckily he did not seem in the mood for one.

"Good afternoon, may we speak with Mr. Chambers?" I asked.

We were shown into the main reception room and were soon joined by Mr. Chambers.

"Good afternoon, gentlemen. How may I help you?" Mr. Chambers asked in a confident tone.

"I am afraid we need to speak to both you and your associate, Mr. Bowles," I responded.

"I'm right here gentlemen," Mr. Bowles said entering the room.

"The Inspector and I are here to place you under arrest," I informed the men.

—

Laughing, Mr. Chambers replied, "What are we under arrest for, we have not done anything wrong."

"For the murder of a local fisherman and for trying to force the daughters of the late Dr. Brown into selling the Bay House to you by terrorizing potential buyers with the story of a Ghost haunting the house," I answered firmly.

The men laughed, "You have no proof to support such wild accusations."

Suddenly the fire that had been burning in the fireplace died. The flames disappeared and all that was left were small embers. The heads of every person within the room turned in shock. What had caused the fire so suddenly to die?

Chapter Seven

Mr. Chambers and Mr. Bowles looked at each other with a puzzled look. From seemingly out of nowhere a voice spoke,

"Perhaps gentlemen, your ghost has turned on you."

The men started to shake in a panic struck manner. They began to move towards the door but they were constrained by a constable who had been posted to make sure the suspects did not get away.

Again the men jumped as an unsuspected noise echoed through the room. It was a loud click and then the creaking of what sounded like a large iron door. I turned towards the fireplace just as my Colonel made a timely entrance through a secret door, which was hidden in the side of the large fireplace.

"Good afternoon, Colonel Simmons," said Inspector Gaunless surprised.

"Good afternoon gentlemen. I apologize for startling you but I want to demonstrate one bit of the evidence, which will prove the guilt of these men. If you would care

—

to take a seat I shall explain to you the answer to the mystery which has haunted this town for some days now," Colonel Simmons said with confidence and a touch of arrogance.

"Certainly Colonel Simmons. It is about time that you explained why we are here," Inspector Gaunless said with a sarcastic tone.

"Well gentlemen, it is quite simple, however clever Mr. Chambers and Mr. Bowles thought they were. As we know Mr. Chambers is the owner of a rather lucrative business, which makes bricks. The grounds of the Bay House have large amounts of the materials needed in the production of bricks. When the Bay House came up for sale after the death of Dr. Brown, Mr. Chambers saw an opportunity to extend his business even further."

"You have no evidence to prove that," interrupted Mr. Chambers.

"Oh, on the contrary Mr. Chambers I do. I could not be certain this was your plan until this morning when I read in the newspaper that you had just recently bought up other areas of land that previously were used for ordnance, just like the land upon which the Bay House is built. Along with this you knew that the council had promised the land to Mr. Bowles at which point you realized that a business arrangement could be drawn up between the two of you. I presume the plan was simple, Mr. Bowles would get the house and Mr. Chambers would get the grounds for his business. I should also imagine that Mr. Bowles was intending to offer Miss Sylvia Brown the opportunity to continue living at the house as long as she agreed to marry him based on the inappropriate advances he had already made towards the young lady.

The problem was how to keep the house from being sold long enough so that the council would rule that it must be sold to Mr. Bowles. That is when the idea of the Ghost came into being. The thought that the Bay House was haunted with a ghost, perhaps even the ghost of the late Dr. Brown, would be enough to scare any potential buyer away. However, what Mr. Bowles and Mr. Chambers did not consider was the curiosity of the local fishermen once the story of the Ghost started to circulate."

"That all makes sense Colonel but how do you

explain the Ghost moving so quickly from one room to another," I asked curiously.

"Ah, I am glad you asked about that, Patterson. Two men created the Ghost, the two stocky men that accompanied Mr. Bowles here today. One would turn on a paraffin lamp in one room and at a set time he would turn his lamp off and the other would light his in a room far removed from the first. Thus the image that the Ghost could move from room to room with relative ease," Colonel Simmons explained.

"A very solid theory so far Colonel Simmons but I need proof that these men were involved before I can arrest them too," stated the Inspector.

"If you look in the Bay House there is plenty of proof that these two men were involved. Firstly, Patterson and I found a spot upon the carpet in one of the rooms that had been stained with paraffin. As I came in through the fireplace I noticed a similar smell as I walked past the two men in question. I am sure that if you examine their sleeves you will also find paraffin stains. I have also noticed distinctive clay and mud on the soles of their shoes, the same clay that I observed in the corridor of the Bay House, several of the rooms there, and the passage that led me here. Inspector, if you take the time to look around the grounds of the Alverbank you will find the soil is mostly made of this specific type of clay."

"And the fisherman?" the Inspector enquired further.

"The fisherman was an unfortunate man caught up in the turn of events, however, without him this mystery may never have been solved. Collins, the fisherman, did not believe that a ghost could exist so he took a closer look. He got too close and for that, sadly, he lost his life. I am sure the plan was for the body to remain in the bread ovens until the house was in the possession of Mr. Bowles, at which point the body could have been disposed of at sea, quietly," Colonel Simmons concluded, with a look of satisfaction on his face. The two men accused looked entirely guilty and their expressions removed all doubt as to their involvement.

"Well, Colonel Simmons, you do seem to have solve the mystery. I do worry that without your timely arrival

—

and curiosity to solve this that these gentlemen would have gotten away with such a horrific scheme," the Inspector exclaimed. Turning towards the door he called out, "Constables, take these men in to custody."

As they were taken from the room Mr. Bowles shouted out,

"It was all his idea! He told us what to do!"

The Inspector thanked Colonel Simmons once more and left the room with the accused. Turning to me, Simmons opened his mouth saying,

"Well Patterson, we have done a good deed here; however, there is still the question of the Bay House and what is to become of it."

Chapter Eight

After the pace of the day Colonel Simmons and I decided to retire to the village tearooms. We took a seat and ordered a pot of tea. Simmons sat quietly reflecting on his success in solving the mystery. His face had a glow to it as clear as the sun. It was obvious to me that he was pleased, in fact it would not be a stretch to say he enjoyed himself. However, it would not be too long before we would have to rejoin the regiment and most likely be posted to some far part of the world.

As much as I felt a sense of joy, the thought that we would soon be leaving this village and returning to the world that I had known for the last eight years, filled me with apprehension. It was not that I hated the Army; however, the days since arriving at the docks in London had shown me what life might be like after the Army. The chances of living in the South after the Army for me were slim. I would of course need a job and I would need to find somewhere to live. I joined the Army at the age of sixteen and without any financial backing starting a life here would be difficult.

—

Colonel Simmons must have seen a disappointed look on my face for he took a sip of his tea and on placing it upon the saucer he asked,

"Is anything the matter Patterson? I would have thought that you would be overflowing with joy at the result of the mystery."

I too took a sip of my tea and then responded,

"I am sir, however, I worry. This has been such a great adventure and yet soon we must return to the regiment."

"This is true Patterson although our destiny as always lies firmly in our hands. You must decide what you wish to do."

"With all due respect sir, that is far more easy for you to do than I."

"That may be but if you could choose anything what would it be?"

I paused a moment and then hesitantly answered,

"Well I… I am not sure sir."

"Oh, do tell, ole boy," Simmons said encouragingly.

"I do not wish to make you feel obliged to act in a particular way as a reaction to what I might wish."

"Oh, I should not feel obliged, Patterson."

"Well then sir, simply put, I wish to stay here. I wish to continue working with you solving crimes and mysteries," I said slightly embarrassed. "However, I realize that it is not a possibility as we must both return to the regiment."

Colonel Simmons took another sip of his tea. Just as he reunited his cup with it's saucer, the door of the tearooms opened. It was Misses Emily and Sylvia Brown.

"What splendid timing," Simmons exclaimed joyfully. "I hope you do not mind but I invited the ladies to join us for a cup of tea."

We both rose from our seats and warmly greeted them. I hung their coats up for them as Colonel Simmons ordered a fresh pot of tea.

"We apologize for our lateness, Colonel Simmons,"

—

Emily said.

"Actually your timing was perfect Miss Brown," Colonel Simmons replied, clearly pleased. "I was just about to announce to Corporal Patterson my plans."

"Your plans, sir?" I asked questioningly, slightly hurt that the ladies were privy to some plans of which I was unaware.

"Yes Patterson, it was already an idea when we arrived in London and upon seeing the newspaper on the quayside I knew that the time was right," Simmons explained.

"Was it the mystery that you saw that furthered your idea," I asked.

"I did see the mystery, however, that was not the part of the newspaper that I have kept in my pocket since that day."

Taking the piece of paper out of his coat pocket he described what was written,

"It was an advertisement that I saw advertising the Bay House. It reads

"The mansion is situated at the western end of Stoke's Bay, immediately opposite the Palace of Osborne and the lawn extends to within fifty yards of high-water mark. The approach to the house is by a handsome drive with Gothic lodges and entrance-gates. A flight of steps lead to the porch, which gives entry to a noble hall, right and left of which are rooms of unusual size and height including a library. The upper storey contains thirty bedrooms. A large garden, which extends from the back of the house, would be amply sufficient to supply the establishment all the year round with fruit and vegetables, while a ten-acre field adjacent to the lawn would furnish a capital playground. Forty acres of land altogether immediately surround the house."

"After reading this I knew it was the place I wanted to settle down. Of course, first there was the question of the ghost and the whole mystery but now that they are solved I can announce my plan. It is my intention to retire my commission as an Army officer and take up residence in this village of Alverstoke. If indeed, Miss Brown you are in agreement I would like to purchase from you the Bay House."

"Why Colonel Simmons, we would be so very grateful and pleased to sell to you the Bay House," Emily

—

Brown exclaimed.

"Splendid! I shall of course pay you the correct amount owed to you for the House and surrounding grounds. I then plan to use it not just as a home but as an office for my business," Colonel Simmons explained. Slightly puzzled I asked of my Colonel,

"And what business will you be undertaking, sir?"

"I intend to follow my passion of puzzle solving. I wish to continue to solve crimes and mysteries just as you so put it Patterson. However, I wish to propose to you an offer Corporal."

Curiously I asked,

"An offer sir?"

"I wish to offer you the position of my assistant, my colleague, my friend. You may have a room and live at the Bay House. Do not feel any pressure to answer now."

"Sir, it would be my honor and my pleasure to continue to work for you," I replied with a sense of gratitude, almost overwhelmed with this new possibility.

"No Patterson, you will not be working for me but with me," Simmons explained.

"Of course."

Delighted by the choices that had been decided, Miss Emily and Sylvia Brown congratulated us and on finishing their cups of tea they gathered their belongings and departed. Colonel Simmons and I were just finishing our tea when Colonel Simmons said to me,

"I should say there is quite a bit of work to do on the House before we can move in."

"Indeed, I should say you are right, sir."

There was a bit of a pause after which the Colonel said,

"Patterson, my name is Edward."

"Edward," I replied in a somewhat nervous tone.

It felt odd to be using the Colonel's Christian name

—

but it felt as if I had somehow gained a wonderful friend. I did not know what the future would bring but, for now, it looked promising.

I handed Colonel Simmons his coat and after putting it on he looked at me with a smile and said,

"Come Patterson, we have not a moment to lose."

Simmons and Patterson will return in

"The Hollow Windmill"

Future titles to look out for in the series include:

'The Hollow Windmill'

'A String of Pearls' and 'The Case of the Faulty Signal'

'The Case of the Jewel Band'

'The Chameleon' and 'The Case of the Big Bang'

'The Four Apers'

'The Disappearing Plates' and 'The Fiery Blanket'

'A Study in Blood'

You can also follow Simmons and Patterson at:

www.simmonsandpatterson.com

www.facebook.com/SimmonsandPatterson

www.twitter.com/SimmsPatt1891

www.carltitterington.anorakpublishing.com

—

20783255R00043

Made in the USA
San Bernardino, CA
23 April 2015